O9-ABI-724

Thomas the Tank Engine & Friends

A BRITT ALLCROFT COMPANY PRODUCTION

Based on The Railway Series by The Rev W Awdry

Visit the Thomas & Friends web site at www.thomasthetankengine.com

ISBN 0-439-33837-9

12 11 10 9 8 7 6 5 4 3 2 1 1 2 3 4 5 6/0

Printed in the U.S.A.
First Scholastic printing, October 2001

by

The REV. W. AWDRY

SCHOLASTIC INC.

New York Toronto London Auckland Sydney
Mexico City New Delhi Hong Kong Buenos Aires

A mob of excited children poured out of Annie and Clarabel one morning and raced down to the beach.

"They're from the Vicar's Sunday School," explained Thomas. "I'm busy this evening, but the Station-Master says I can ask you to take them home."

"Of course I will," promised Percy.

The children had a lovely day. But at tea time it got very hot. Dark clouds loomed overhead. Then came lightning, thunder, and rain. The children only just managed to reach shelter before the deluge began.

Annie and Clarabel stood at the platform. The children scrambled in.

"Can we go home please, Station-Master?" asked the Vicar.

The Station-Master called Percy. "Take the children home quickly, please," he ordered.

The rain streamed down on Percy's boiler. "Ugh!" he shivered, and thought of his nice dry shed. Then he remembered.

"A promise is a promise," he told himself, "so here goes."

His Driver was anxious. The river was rising fast. It foamed and swirled fiercely, threatening to flood the countryside any minute.

6

The rain beat on Percy's face. "I wish I could see—I wish I could see," he complained.

They left a cutting and found themselves in water. "Oooh, my wheels!" shivered Percy. "It's cold!" But he struggled on.

"*Oooooooooooooshshshshshsh!*" he hissed. "It's sloshing my fire."

They stopped and backed the coaches to the cutting and waited while the Guard found a telephone.

He returned looking gloomy. "We couldn't go back if we wanted to," he said, "the bridge near the junction is down."

The Fireman went to the Guard's coach, carrying a hatchet.

"Hullo!" said the Guard, "you look fierce."

"I want some dry wood for Percy's fire, please."

They broke up some boxes, but that did not satisfy the Fireman. "I need some of your floor boards, too," he told the Guard.

"What! My nice floor?" grumbled the Guard. "I only swept it this morning." But he still helped.

Soon, they had plenty of wood stored in Percy's bunker. His fire was burning well now. He felt warm and comfortable again.

"Buzzzzzzzzzzz! Buzzzzzzzzzzzzz! Buzzzzzzzzzzzzzzzzz!"

Oh, dear! thought Percy sadly. Harold helicopter's come to laugh at me.

Bump! Something thudded onto Percy's boiler. "Ow!" he exclaimed in a muffled voice. "That's really not nice! He shouldn't throw things."

His Driver unwound a parachute from Percy's indignant front. "Harold isn't throwing things at you," he laughed. "He's dropping hot drinks for us."

They all had a drink of cocoa and felt better.

Percy had steam up now. "*Peep peep!* Thank you, Harold!" he whistled. "Come on, let's go."

The water lapped his wheels. "Ugh!" he shivered. It crept up and up and up. It reached his ash pan, then it sloshed at his fire.

"*Oooooooooooooshshshshshshshshshsh!*" Percy was losing steam, but he plunged bravely on. "I promised," he panted, "I promised."

The Driver and Fireman piled his fire high with wood and managed to keep him steaming.

"I *must* do it," he gasped, "I must, I must, I must."

He made a last great effort and stood, exhausted but triumphant, on rails that were clear of the flood.

He rested to get steam back, then brought the train home.

"Three cheers for Percy!" called the Vicar, and the children nearly raised the roof!

Sir Topham Hatt arrived in Harold. First he thanked the men. "Harold told me you were a wizard, Percy. He says he can beat you at some things . . ."

Percy snorted.

". . . but *not* at being a submarine." He chuckled. "I don't know what you've both been playing at, and I won't ask! But I do know that you're a Really Useful Engine."

"Oh, Sir!" whispered Percy happily.

Now flip the book over to start another Thomas & Friends adventure.

6

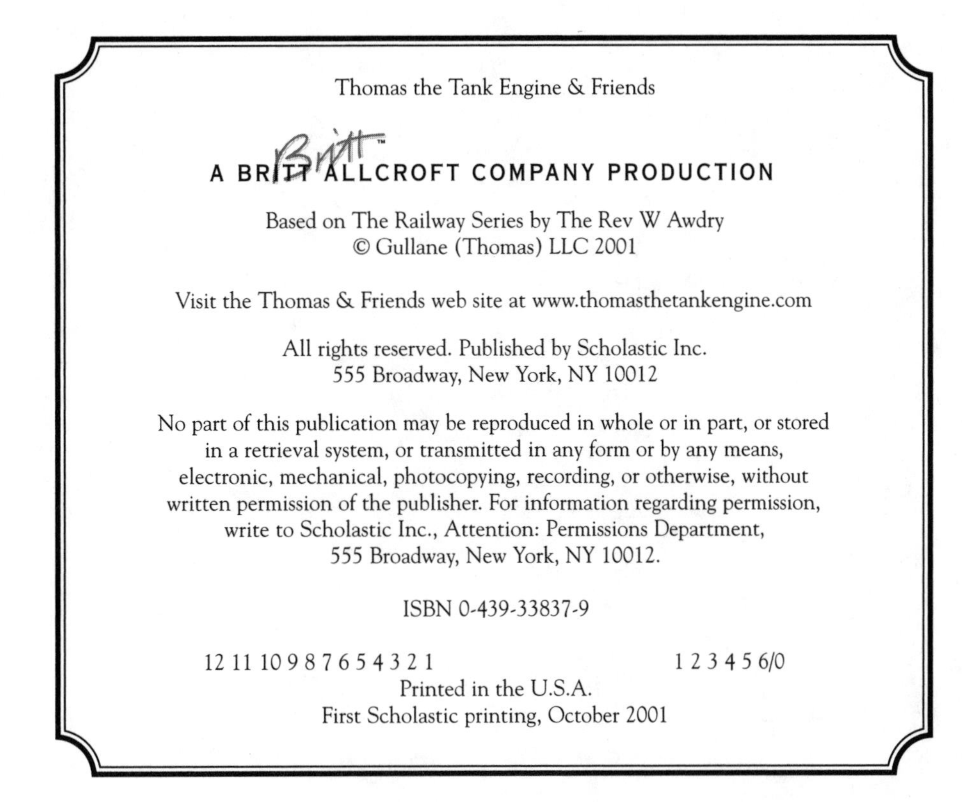

Thomas the Tank Engine & Friends

A BRITT ALLCROFT COMPANY PRODUCTION

Based on The Railway Series by The Rev W Awdry

Visit the Thomas & Friends web site at www.thomasthetankengine.com

 Published by Scholastic Inc.
555 Broadway, New York, NY 10012

ISBN 0-439-33837-9

12 11 10 9 8 7 6 5 4 3 2 1 1 2 3 4 5 6/0

Printed in the U.S.A.

First Scholastic printing, October 2001

PERCY Takes the Plunge

by

The REV. W. AWDRY

SCHOLASTIC INC.

New York Toronto London Auckland Sydney
Mexico City New Delhi Hong Kong Buenos Aires

Sometimes Percy takes freight cars full of stones to the other end of the line. There, he meets engines from the Other Railway.

One day, Henry wanted to rest in the shed, but Percy was talking to some tank engines.

". . . It was raining hard. Water swirled under my boiler. I couldn't see where I was going, but I struggled on."

"Ooooh Percy, you *are* brave."

"Well," said Percy modestly, "it wasn't anything really. Water's nothing to an engine with determination."

"Tell us more, Percy," said the engines.

"What are you engines doing here?" hissed Henry. "This shed is for Sir Topham Hatt's engines. Go away."

"Silly things," Henry snorted.

"They're not silly." Percy had been enjoying himself. He was cross because Henry had sent them away.

"They are silly, and so are you. 'Water's nothing to an engine with determination.' Pah!"

"Anyway," said cheeky Percy, "I'm not afraid of water. I like it." He ran away singing,

"Once an engine attached to a train
Was afraid of a few drops of rain . . ."

Percy arrived home feeling pleased with himself. "Silly old Henry," he chuckled.

Thomas was looking at a sign on the quay. It said DANGER.

"We mustn't go past it," Thomas said. "That's orders."

"Why?"

" '*DANGER*' means falling down something," said Thomas. "I went past '*DANGER*' once and fell down a mine."

Percy looked beyond the sign. "I can't see a mine," he said. He didn't know that the foundations of the quay had sunk, and that the rails now sloped downward to the sea.

DANGER
6

"Silly sign!" said Percy. For days and days, he tried to sneak past it, but his Driver stopped him every time.

"No, you don't," he would say.

Then Percy made a plan.

One day at the top station, he whispered to the freight cars, "Will you give me a bump when we get to the quay?"

The freight cars were surprised. They had never been asked to bump an engine before. They giggled and chattered about it the whole way down.

"Whoa Percy! Whoa!" said his Driver, and Percy slowed down obediently at the distant signal.

"Driver doesn't know my plan," he chuckled.

"On! On! On!" laughed the freight cars.

Percy thought they were helping. "I'll pretend to stop at the station, but the freight cars will push me past the sign. Then I'll make them stop. I can do that whenever I like."

If Percy hadn't been so conceited, he would never have been so silly. Every wise engine knows that you cannot trust freight cars.

6

They reached the station, and Percy's brakes groaned. That was the signal for the freight cars.

"Go on! Go on!" they yelled and surged forward together.

They gave Percy a fearful bump and knocked his Driver and Fireman off the footplate.

"Ow!" said Percy, sliding past the sign.

The day was misty. The rails were slippery. His wheels wouldn't grip.

Percy was frantic. "That's enough!" he hissed.

But it was too late. Once on the slope, he tobogganed helplessly down, crashed through the buffers, and slithered into the sea.

"You are a very disobedient engine."

Percy knew that voice. He groaned. The foreman had borrowed a small boat and rowed Sir Topham Hatt around.

"Please, Sir, get me out Sir, I'm truly sorry Sir."

"No, Percy, we cannot do that till high tide. I hope it will teach you to obey orders."

"Yes, Sir." Percy shivered miserably. He was cold. Fish were playing hide and seek through his wheels. The tide rose higher and higher.

He was feeling his position more and more deeply every minute.

It was nearly dark when they brought floating cranes, cleared away the freight cars, and lifted Percy out. He was too cold and stiff to move by himself, so he was sent to the Works the next day on Henry's goods train.

"Well! Well! Well!" chuckled Henry, "Did you like the water?"

"No."

"I *am* surprised. You need more determination, Percy. 'Water's nothing to an engine with determination' you know. Perhaps you will like it better next time."

But Percy was quite determined that there wouldn't be a "next time."

Now flip the book over to start another Thomas & Friends adventure.